Annie Was Warned

Jarrett J. Krosoczka

Dragonfly Books ━➤ New York

On Halloween night,

Annie sneaked out to the creepy old Montgomery mansion.

Annie's parents told her not to go.
"It's got bats," they warned.
    "Bats don't scare me!" Annie said.

Annie's big sister said she
should stay away.
"It's full of creepy spiders,"
she cautioned.
    "I like spiders." Annie smiled.

Annie's friend James nodded.
"That place is haunted, all right,"
he said with a shudder.
Then he grinned. "I *dare* you to go!"

Annie was warned . . .

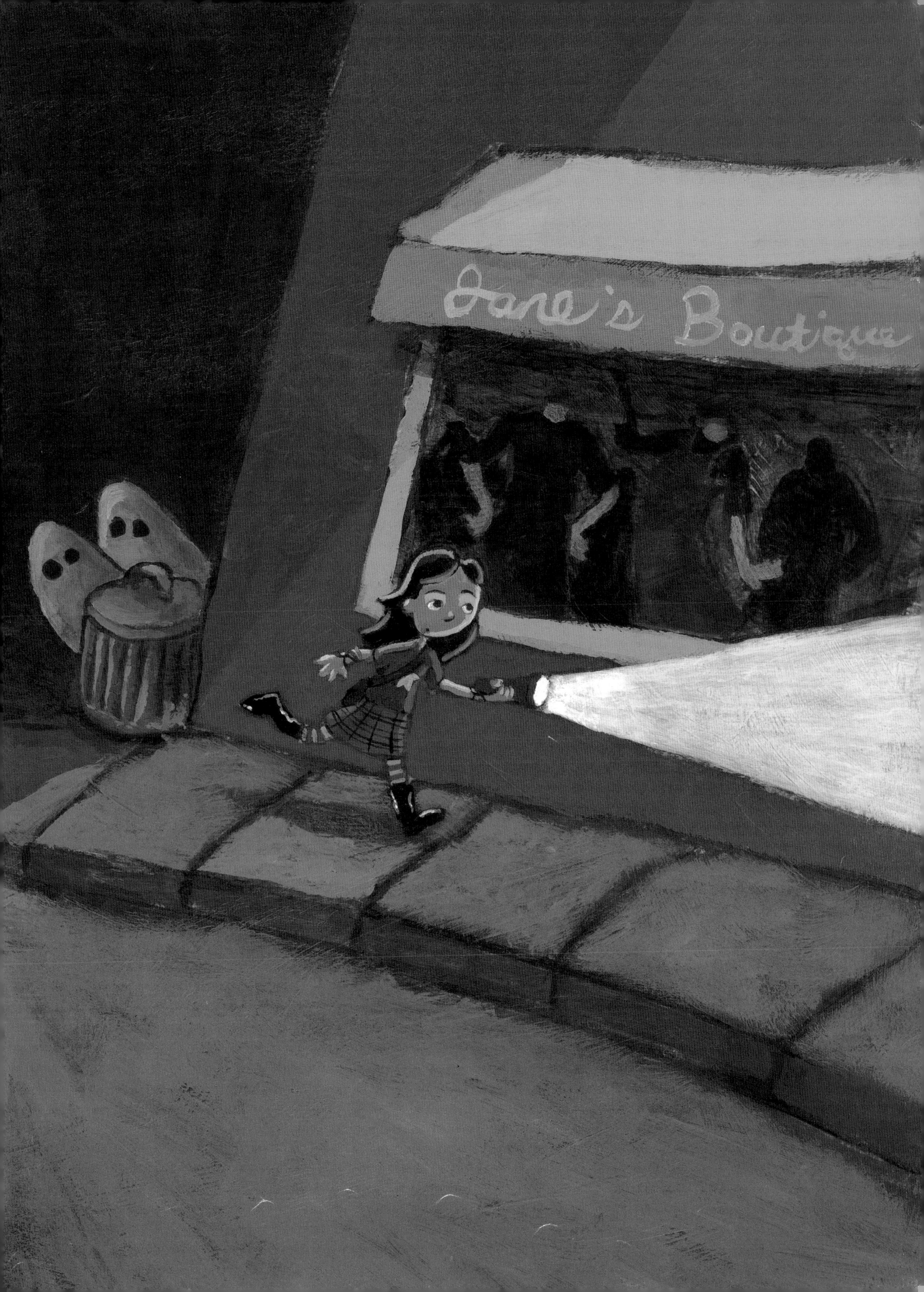
Jane's Boutique

...but Annie wasn't scared.

She stole down the quiet street.
The moon was shining. The wind was howling.
The tall trees swayed in the breeze.
But Annie wasn't afraid of anything!
After all, she was born on Halloween night.

Out of the corner of her eye, she saw something black fly by!

Was it a bat?

But there was only a cat, licking its paws.

Annie turned the corner and crept
across the churchyard.
Something tickled the back of her neck!

Was it a spider?

Annie spun around.
It was just the leaves falling from the trees.

The mansion loomed large in the night.
Annie thought she heard whispers.

Was it haunted?

SCRAY

Annie took a deep breath
and began to climb the stairs.

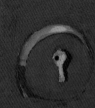

It was the best scare
she'd ever had.

FOR MY SISTER,
MAURA

A SPECIAL ACKNOWLEDGMENT TO ANN RITTER AND HER INDELIBLE SENSE OF STYLE

Copyright © 2003 by Jarrett J. Krosoczka • All rights reserved. Published in the United States by Dragonfly Books, an imprint of Random House Children's Books, a division of Random House, Inc., New York. Originally published in hardcover in the United States by Alfred A. Knopf, New York, in 2003. • Dragonfly Books with the colophon is a registered trademark of Random House, Inc. • Visit us on the Web! randomhouse.com/kids • Educators and librarians, for a variety of teaching tools, visit us at RHTeachersLibrarians.com • The Library of Congress has cataloged the hardcover edition of this work as follows: Krosoczka, Jarrett. • Annie was warned / by Jarrett J. Krosoczka. — 1st ed. • p. cm. • Summary: Disregarding warnings about the creepy mansion outside of town, Annie bravely goes to investigate on Halloween night and gets a big surprise. • ISBN 978-0-375-81567-6 (trade) — ISBN 978-0-375-91567-3 (lib. bdg.) — ISBN 978-0-375-98375-7 (ebook) • [1. Haunted houses–Fiction. 2. Halloween–Fiction. 3. Surprise–Fiction. 4. Birthdays–Fiction.] I. Title. • PZ7.K935An 2003 [E]–dc21 2002043280 • ISBN 978-0-385-75341-8 (pbk.) • MANUFACTURED IN CHINA • 10 9 8 7 6 5 4 3 2 1 • First Dragonfly Books Edition • Random House Children's Books supports the First Amendment and celebrates the right to read.